LEGO STAR WARS™

THE OFFICIAL STORMTROOPER TRAINING MANUAL

ADVANCED GUIDE TO THE GALAXY

Story by
Arie Kaplan

Scholastic Inc.

For Aviya Leah Kaplan, the greatest Padawan
(and the greatest daughter) in the entire galaxy.

LEGO, the
LEGO logo, the Brick and
Knob configurations and the Minifigure
are trademarks of/ sont des marques de commerce
du the LEGO Group. © 2017 The LEGO Group. Produced by
Scholastic Inc. under license from The LEGO Group.

© & ™ Lucasfilm Ltd.

ISBN 978-0-545-92542-6

10 9 8 7 6 5 4 3 2 1   17 18 19 20 21

Printed in China   95
First printing 2017

THE OFFICIAL STORMTROOPER TRAINING MANUAL: YOUR GUIDE TO STORMING LIKE A TROOPER!

INTRODUCTION

Congratulations! If you're holding this employee handbook, that means you're now a proud member of the Stormtrooper Corps, the elite force that serves the Galactic Empire. But don't get too excited! You still have a lot to learn.

This book is a guide to all of the different types of stormtroopers, as well as their armor, weaponry, and vehicles. It will inspire your work as a stormtrooper. Or as Emperor Palpatine might say, it will "Feed your anger! Make you stronger!"

STORMTROOPERS

They are the Imperial stormtroopers, the peacekeepers of the spaceways. Always battle-ready and clad in their signature white armor, they're the only things keeping the galaxy from toppling into total chaos. And they are totally not clumsy and disorganized, no matter what lies you've been told.

Okay, so sometimes stormtroopers have been known to, er . . . bungle things like "marksmanship." Or "stealth." Or "doing their jobs right." But they look good in white armor, okay? They're cool. Stormtroopers are cool. So there.

STORMTROOPER HELMETS

Reinforced helmet also doubles as a car seat for the little ones!

Black lenses mean they never see you cry—er, sweat!

Nozzles supply the helmet's interior with air, and also with a nice potpourri scent.

STORMTROOPER ARMOR

These bad boys rock fully tricked-out body armor boasting cool features, like:

It's impervious to projectile weapons— but not mean insults.

Knee protection plate, so you can get down on one knee to fire your blaster (or to propose to your special stormtrooper lady friend . . . HINT HINT!).

The little thing that looks like a glued-on domino is the manual suit control unit. Unless you're a truly hopeless stormtrooper, in which case it's . . . a glued-on domino. Sorry!

STORMTROOPER ARMOR

Utility belt, which contains survival equipment, temperature controls, and nachos.

Eighteen-piece plastoid-composite armor . . . which will do you no good against a Wookiee, a Hutt, and whatever the heck Nien Nunb is.

STORMTROOPER WEAPONS

The DLT-20A blaster rifle is the stormtrooper's sidearm of choice.

Its power cell carries enough energy for 100 shots, all with really cool *"Pew! Pew! Pew!"* sound effects.

Features an advanced cooling system, making it literally the "coolest weapon ever."

AT-AT

AT-ATs can move on all kinds of land. They can move across jungles, oceans, or (if you're a super LAZY stormtrooper) couches. They're supposed to be "all-terrain," but I've never seen one walking around in outer space. Just saying . . .

The AT-AT is often the first thing sent into a combat zone. The LAST thing sent into a combat zone is a stormtrooper named "Shirtless Lou," who has the words WE WON painted on his belly.

The AT-AT also has very dense armor. But whenever I say that, some new recruit pipes up: "Not as dense as a stormtrooper, am I right?"

AT-ATs are armed with two head-mounted laser cannons. Those cannons are mounted on the heads of the vehicle, not on the heads of the stormtroopers.

Its heavy feet are also good at flattening enemy troops . . . a maneuver known as "making rebel pancakes."

STAR DESTROYER

Star Destroyers are called that because they are capable of destroying whole star systems. Here are a few other "Star Destroyer Specs":

Ships shaped like daggers are known as "Star Destroyers." Ships shaped like butter knives are known as "nonthreatening."

The command tower is where you can say cool stuff like, "Destroy that star!" and "Truly, this is a Star Destroyer we are standing inside of right now."

Star Destroyers are generally classified as being between 1,000 to 2,000 meters in length. In other words, they're big enough to hold two or three Hutts.

REPUBLIC ATTACK GUNSHIPS

The Republic Attack Gunships (a ship type that is no longer used), also known as Low-Altitude Assault Transport/infantry (LAAT/i), were vessels used to transport clone troopers to places they were needed, which seemed to be pretty much everywhere, as wars seemed to be breaking out all across the stars. It was a constant series of "star wars," if you will. Some additional info on these gunships:

Ships that predate the Empire, Republic Attack Gunships transported infantry, which (contrary to how it sounds) does not mean a bunch of infants. It means soldiers. Weird, huh?

THE DEATH STAR

Millions of stormtroopers work at the Death Star. Millions. I mean, it's the size of a moon, right? Frankly, we didn't know what section to put it in: Is it a vehicle or a weapon? Both, kinda. But one thing we do know: You do not wanna mess with it. Honestly, you'd have to be a clueless farm boy from a backwater planet like Tatooine in order to mess with it.

This fully armed and operational battle station includes such features as . . .

Conference room. 'Cause you know how you become the scourge of the galaxy? By having meetings, y'all! Wooooo, scary!

A trash compactor. The Emperor sometimes talks to it: "Compact your trash! Gives you focus! Makes you stronger!"

Detention block, which . . . well, let's just say it's not the kind of "detention" where you stay after school!

It possesses firepower unequaled in the history of warfare. But also? One heck of a soda machine!

SNOWTROOPERS

Snowtroopers are special stormtroopers who are equipped to move about in frigid environments, like the icy planet Hoth. Snowtroopers are also prone to asking, "Is it hot in here or is it just me?" when they're in any room where the temperature is above freezing.

The Empire handpicks snowtroopers from worlds with a chilly climate. This way, they can be sent out into the freezing cold, but they won't be slowed down by the elements. And they can point the way to really good ice cream shops.

SNOWTROOPER ARMOR

Each snowtrooper wears a rugged body glove, which insulates him from the cold. It also makes him look like a big ol' oven mitt.

Hidden compartment for storing hot cocoa.

The chest plate houses the snowtroopers' life-support systems, and also plays holovids of *Coruscant's Got Talent.*

A "breather hood" helps the snowtrooper function in freezing weather. And it's usually the "ghost costume" they wear to the Empire's annual costume ball.

Button-on snowtrooper armor that makes snow cones. But do you know what snowtroopers are sick to death of? Snow cones. (Or anything snow-related, for that matter.)

Snowtrooper armor enables its wearer to survive in a brutal, frigid climate, and also make great snow angels.

SCOUT TROOPERS

Scout troopers, also known as biker scouts, are trained for activities too complex for regular stormtroopers, such as spy craft, marksmanship, and making exact change. They are known for being particularly rude, selfish, and obnoxious—in other words, just really good stormtroopers.

Despite their skills, some of the Empire's finest scout troopers have been defeated by running into trees. So, go figure.

SCOUT TROOPER ARMOR

Scout troopers' armor is lighter than normal stormtrooper armor, making them great fighters, and even better dancers.

Their helmets are equipped with enhanced goggles, which let them see things super close up. So they can tell if you spilled lunch on yourself.

Because of their white armor, scout troopers stand out like a sore thumb in an environment that has a lot of color. In other words, anywhere.

The mouthpieces on scout troopers' helmets resemble gumball machines, but they are not actual gumball machines. If you don't believe that, just stick a coin in there and see what happens.

Their field kits come with food and supplies, but surprisingly, they do NOT come with a FIELD.

Their kneepads serve them well when on missions, and also when playing space hockey.

IMPERIAL SPEEDER BIKE

The 74-Z speeder bike is most frequently used by scout troopers, which is why they're also called "biker scouts." Good thing it wasn't called the "speeder thingy," 'cause "thingy scouts" sounds really silly.

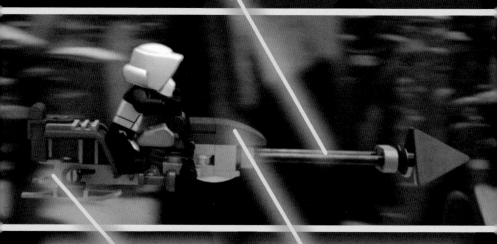

Comes with a "my kid is an Imperial honor student" bumper sticker.

Yes, you can get a bike horn for the speeder bike. But speeder bikes are supposed to be scary, and how scary is a bike horn?

CLONE TROOPERS

Clone troopers were exact genetic duplicates of one another. They were raised in a laboratory and grown at an accelerated rate. You may think that description also fits those annoying quadruplets you were forced to bunk with at summer camp, but this is something else entirely.

The clone troopers were an army of soldiers who were created to serve in the Grand Army of the Republic during the conflict that was eventually known as the Clone Wars. They used to serve the Jedi, but don't hold that against them. After all, nobody's perfect. After the Clone Wars, Emperor Palpatine replaced the clone troopers with "Imperial stormtroopers." So yeah, these guys were the first stormtroopers. Think of them like your ancestors. Your creepy, totally identical ancestors.

CLONE TROOPER ARMOR

Clone troopers could attach sun visors and binoculars to their helmets. Some could even attach propeller beanies, but those weren't regulation.

Clone trooper battle armor featured a T-shaped visor, because the Q-shaped visor just looked really not cool.

The first Phase I clone officers used colors to distinguish themselves. Commanders were marked by yellow stripes, captains were identified by red stripes, and troopers who like Neapolitan ice cream were marked by strawberry, vanilla, and chocolate stripes.

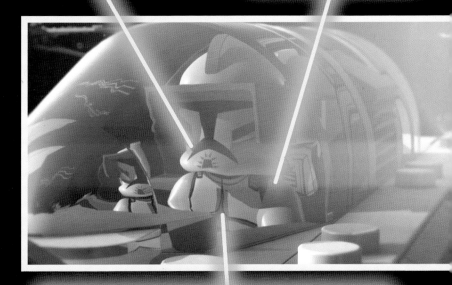

CLONE TROOPER WEAPONS

Clone trooper weapons included blaster rifles and blaster carbines. Can you tell that clone troopers were super into blasters?

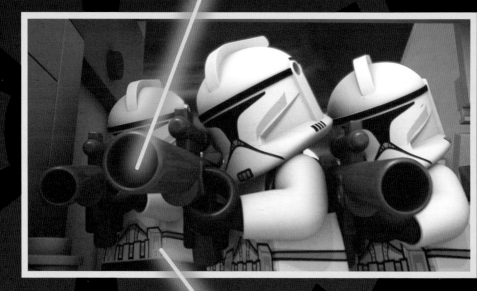

Clone troopers carried various types of grenades, such as haywire grenades, electromagnetic pulse grenades, and the much rarer "slight headache grenades."

Being a stormtrooper is a great way to meet people. In the next few pages, we'll cover some famous figures from history, and the awesome people you might encounter while serving the Empire. They're totally laid-back, chill people, and they totally aren't making me say this. Nope. Totally not. At all.

GENERAL GRIEVOUS

Grievous was the galaxy's second-most-famous rampaging cyborg with serious lightsaber skills and even more serious shortness of breath.

General Grievous used to hunt down Jedi and collect their lightsabers. Because coin collecting was just TOO dull for him.

During the Clone Wars, General Grievous's official title was "Supreme Commander of the Droid Army of the Confederacy of Independent Systems." Or as Count Dooku called him, "Hey, you!"

DARTH MAUL

Darth Maul was just your average tattoo lover/Sith Lord. Here are some things you should know about him:

Darth Maul had several cranial horns poking out of his head. They were good for frightening enemies, and for impersonating a reindeer.

Darth Maul had a lightsaber with a blade at both ends. Wanna guess how many times he forgot to grip it in the middle? (Answer: a lot.)

BOBA FETT

A mysterious bounty hunter working for Darth Vader, Boba Fett lives by his own rules. Unfortunately, those rules apparently don't include showering very often.

His jetpack has a device that launches rockets, grenades, and fireworks (when he's feeling festive).

Boba's arsenal includes an ion cannon, which shoots . . . we don't know, ions?

Boba is the only unaltered clone of the famed bounty hunter Jango Fett.

Boba inherited his ship, *Slave I*, from his father, Jango Fett, who was just like Boba, only LESS cuddly. *Slave I* boasts the following Fett-approved features:

A concussion missile launcher and a cruise missile launcher (which, oddly enough, does not take people on cruises).

A homing beacon (not "homing bacon"—some stormtroopers have made that mistake).

A jamming array, which makes the ship invisible (it also plays music for when Boba wants to jam).

COUNT DOOKU

A former Jedi, Count Dooku was a Sith Lord.
His Sith name was Darth Tyranus. His rap
name was MC Eyebrows. Other Dooku details:

Dooku scowled a lot. He used to have other facial expressions,
but he had them surgically removed.

Dooku's lightsaber had a curved hilt
that allowed for precise movements,
especially when he used it to cut the
crusts off of sandwiches.

As a Sith Lord, Dooku was great at
swordplay, strategy, and kneeling
before dudes in hooded capes.

JABBA THE HUTT

Jabba the Hutt, also known as "His Royal Wideness" (though never to his face), is one of the most notorious crime lords in the galaxy. Here are a few other things about this massively fearful (and just plain massive) gangster:

Jabba lives in a castle on a planet covered in sand. Oddly enough, it's not a sand castle.

Jabba the Hutt is the leader of the Desilijic kajidic, a totally legitimate business, and anyone who says otherwise is a big liar!

Jabba has many priorities, such as power, wealth, and lunch.

DARTH VADER

He's the Big EnchilaDarth. He's Sith-ly Irresistible. He's . . . probably going to Force-push me if I make another awful pun. He's Darth Vader. Here's some Darth deets:

Because the mouth-plate on his breathing mask has very narrow slats, he can only eat whatever he can slurp through a straw. So Lord Vader gets VERY cranky if we don't pack his sippy cup!

Darth Vader really likes to be an invader. And if he doesn't invade something or someone after a couple days? Total chaos. (Even worse if he's ALSO lost the sippy cup.)

Vader is powered by anger, grumpiness, and two AA batteries.

THE EMPEROR

Meet Emperor Palpatine, who should win some sort of award for most intimidating bathrobe. Here are a few pointers about Palpatine:

Before he created the Death Star, Palpatine experimented with various other super-weapons, including the Death Cloud, the Death Moon, and the Death Rainbow.

Palpatine's full name is actually "Sheev Palpatine." Not to be confused with "Steve Palpatine," intergalactic plumber-extraordinaire.

We can honestly say Emperor Palpatine is the nicest emperor (who dresses like he's getting ready for the shower and looks like a white toad) that we've ever met.

In conclusion . . .

This concludes our stormtrooper handbook. We hope that you've found it educational, informative, and maybe even a little bit inspirational. As you are ushered into the distinguished ranks of the Stormtrooper Corps, always remember that we are a solemn, serious organization, and—OW!

Flip to the activity section to test your stormtrooper skills!

BEGIN COMMUNICATION:
IMPRESSIVE! YOU'VE MADE IT THROUGH THE GUIDE BOOK SECTION WITH SITH-
LIKE SPEED! NOW BEHOLD THE MIGHT OF THIS FULLY ARMED AND OPERATIONAL
ACTIVITY SECTION, PACKED WITH TRAINING EXERCISES CLEVERLY DISGUISED AS
"GAMES" AND "ACTIVITIES" THAT WILL GAUGE WHETHER YOU TRULY HAVE WHAT
IT TAKES TO BE A STORMTROOPER. IF YOU DON'T HAVE WHAT IT TAKES, IT IS
ASSUMED THAT YOU ARE PART OF THE REBEL ALLIANCE AND A TRAITOR! (BUT
YOU'RE PROBABLY NOT, RIGHT? RIGHT?!)

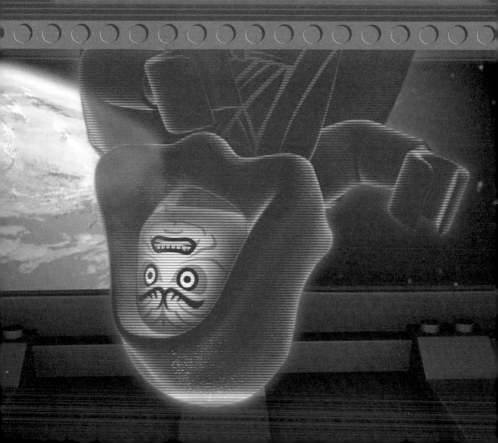

PERHAPS YOU THINK YOU'RE BEING TREATED UNFAIRLY? THAT THIS IS 'JUST AN ACTIVITY SECTION'? JUST "FUN AND GAMES"? WELL, THE EMPEROR DOESN'T THINK SO. STAY ON TARGET. USE ANY MEANS NECESSARY TO FINISH ALL OF THE ACTIVITIES IN THIS BOOK. THAT IS ALL.

END COMMUNICATION

ACTIVITIES!

MY STORMTROOPER HOBBIES

_____

_____

_____

_____

_____

_____

_____

_____

_____

_____

MAKE YOUR OWN STORMTROOPER TO-DO LIST

WHEN YOU FIRST JOINED THE HONORABLE RANKS OF THE IMPERIAL STORMTROOPERS, YOUR LIFE CHANGED. NOW ORDER AND DISCIPLINE IS EVERYTHING, AND YOUR SCHEDULE IS VERY ORGANIZED. YOU'RE MAKING DAILY (IF NOT HOURLY) TO-DO LISTS. HERE'S AN EXAMPLE OF ONE OF YOUR COLLEAGUE'S LISTS:

☐ 8 a.m.: Wake up. Pick up HoloNewspaper from driveway. Tell paperboy to "Move along, move along . . ."

☐ 10 a.m.: Shoot at something, miss the target entirely.

☐ 2 p.m.: Buy NEW suits of completely identical white armor.

☐ 6 p.m.: Tell travel agent that the cloud of dark matter in deep space she booked for our vacation is "not the void we're looking for."

WHAT'S ON YOUR TO-DO LIST?
FILL IT IN ON THE NEXT PAGE . . .

_____ ☐

_____ ☐

_____ ☐

_____ ☐

_____ ☐

_____ ☐

_____ ☐

_____ ☐

_____ ☐

_____ ☐

STORMTROOPER TO-DO LIST

MYSTERIOUS MISSING LETTERS

THIS DOCUMENT WAS LEFT UNFINISHED BY ONE OF YOUR, ER ... LESS-THAN-
SKILLED FELLOW STORMTROOPERS. FILL IN THE BLANKS TO COMPLETE THE
NAMES OF THESE NOTORIOUS REBELS AND ENEMIES OF THE EMPIRE:

H _ _ A   Z _ B

_ ZR _   _ AN _ N

S _ B _ N   _ HO _ _ ER

100% EMPIRE-APPROVED, IMPERIALLY SANCTIONED JOKES

EMPEROR PALPATINE FOUND THEM FUNNY AND SO SHOULD YOU! (SERIOUSLY; PLEASE LAUGH AT THESE JOKES OR YOU WILL BE HELD IN A DETAINMENT CELL ON SUSPICION OF SYMPATHIZING WITH THE REBEL ALLIANCE. BECAUSE ANYONE WHO DOESN'T FIND THESE JOKES FUNNY IS PART OF THE REBEL ALLIANCE AND A TRAITOR!)

Q: What vegetables do Jedi eat?

A: Obi-Wan KenoBEETS

Q: What happened when the rebels and the Empire played one another in a baseball game?

A: The umpire struck back

Q: What do you call a princess who can't fall asleep?

A: Princess Leia-wake at night

Q: What do you call 2,000 Jedi sucked into a black hole?

A: A good start

Q: What vehicle does Lord Vader fly when he's feeling casual?

A: A No-TIE Fighter

Q: What vehicle does Lord Vader fly when he's feeling fancy?

A: A Bow-TIE Fighter

STORMTROOPER SNACKING

WHAT SORT OF FOODS DO YOU LIKE? ARE
THERE ANY FOODS YOU ENJOY COOKING?
WRITE A LIST OF YOUR FAVORITE FOODS AND
SUBMIT IT TO YOUR COMMANDING OFFICER.
(AFTER ALL, YOU MAY HAVE TO COOK DINNER
FOR YOUR WHOLE PLATOON SOMEDAY!)

WAUUGH!

FINISH THE MISSION REPORT

WHEN YOU AND ONE OF YOUR FELLOW STORMTROOPERS WERE ON A RECENT MISSION, YOUR ARMORED ALLY GOT BOPPED ON THE NOGGIN BY AN ANGRY WOOKIEE. AFTERWARD, YOUR FRIEND TRIED TO GIVE HIS OFFICIAL MISSION REPORT TO HIS COMMANDING OFFICER. BUT AS A RESULT OF HIS WOOKIEE ENCOUNTER, HE HAD TROUBLE REMEMBERING ALL THE SPECIFICS. SINCE YOU WERE ON THE MISSION WITH HIM, CAN YOU HELP HIM OUT BY FILLING IN THE BLANKS ON THE NEXT PAGE?

We had just touched down on a planet called
_____.

It was a place filled with the most
horrendous-looking _____ we had ever seen.

So the first thing we did was borrow a _____
and use it to travel to the _____. Once there,

a bounty hunter named

_____ came

after us, insisting that

we had stolen his buried

_____.

SUM-TROOPER

A STORMTROOPER'S MIND NEEDS TO ALWAYS BE SHARP, LIKE EMPEROR PALPATINE'S FINGERNAILS. TO STRENGTHEN YOUR MENTAL SKILLS, MAKE YOUR WAY THROUGH THIS MATHEMATICAL MESS. IN THE LINES BELOW, PLACE NUMBERS 2, 4, 6, 8, AND 10 SO THAT EACH LINE ADDS UP TO 20. CAN YOU DO IT?

$13 + \underline{} + 3 = 20$

$\underline{} + \underline{} + \underline{} = 20$

$9 + \underline{} + 5 = 20$

THE DEATH STAR CAFETERIA MENU

THESE ARE SOME OF THE CAFETERIA ITEMS YOUR FELLOW STORMTROOPERS EAT EVERY DAY:

- BOBA FETA CHEESE

- LANDO CALZONE

- DARTH WAFER

- YODA YOGURT

- BLUE MILK SHAKE

- GENERAL GRIEVOUS GRILLED CHEESE

- DARK LORD OF THE (BARBECUE) SPIT

- A "JAR JAR" OF DRINKS

- A WRETCHED HIVE OF CRUMBS
  & VANILLA BEANS

- HAN SALAD

- THE DEATH STAR RAW BAR

- TRADE BLOCKADE STACKADE OF PANCAKES

TROOPER TRIVIA!

NO STORMTROOPER CAN JOIN UNLESS THEY KNOW SOMETHING ABOUT THE HISTORY OF OUR GLORIOUS EMPIRE. SO WE KNOW YOU WON'T MIND IF WE ASK YOU TO ANSWER A FEW IMPERIAL TRIVIA QUESTIONS. AFTER YOU FINISH EACH ONE, JUST MOVE ALONG NOW, MOVE ALONG (TO THE NEXT PAGE).

1) The original wave of clone troopers were all genetic clones of:

A) Darth Gary

B) Jango Fett

C) Qui-Gon Jim

D) Jabba the Hutt

2) Stormtrooper commander armor has something that makes it impervious to many attacks. What is it?

A) Superhero cape

B) Shark repellent

C) Good luck charm

D) Built-in shield generator

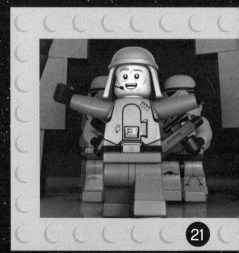

3) All Imperial stormtroopers are completely loyal to:
A) Emperor Fred
B) Emperor Palpatine
C) Count Dracula
D) Count Dooku

4) During an actual storm, a stormtrooper will:
A) Gain storm-based superpowers
B) Run and seek shelter from the storm
C) Study the storm and take notes
D) Do absolutely nothing weird

5) Which of the following is NOT the name of an actual Sith Lord:

A) Darth Tyranus
B) Darth Sidious
C) Darth Nastyus
D) Darth Vader

6) Clone SCUBA troopers were grown on which planet:

A) Kamino
B) Casino
C) Vega
D) Aquatica

DECODE THE REBELLION!

WE HAVE INTERCEPTED A HIDDEN MESSAGE FROM THE REBELS IN THAT TANGLE OF WORDS ON THE NEXT PAGE. YOUR MISSION IS TO SOLVE IT! UNSCRAMBLE THE WORDS ON THE NEXT PAGE AND WRITE THEM IN THE SPACE PROVIDED.

CBWCHEACA DNESE ENW RFU HAOSMPO!
—HNA OOSL

_ _ _ _ _ _ _ _ _   _ _ _ _ _

_ _ _   _ _ _   _ _ _ _ _ _ _ !

_ _ _ _   _ _ _ _

STORMTROOPER POETRY

STORMTROOPERS AREN'T KNOWN FOR THEIR POETRY, MAINLY BECAUSE IT'S HARD TO TALK WHILE WEARING A HELMET OVER YOUR FACE. BUT THAT DOESN'T MEAN THAT THEY DON'T WRITE POETRY. THEY WRITE EVERYTHING FROM LIMERICKS TO HAIKU. A HAIKU IS A FORM OF THREE-LINE POETRY WITH A SIMPLE STRUCTURE: FIVE SYLLABLES FOR THE FIRST LINE, THEN SEVEN SYLLABLES FOR THE SECOND LINE, THEN FIVE ONCE MORE FOR THE THIRD LINE. ON THE FOLLOWING PAGE, HERE ARE SOME OF THE HAIKU STORMTROOPERS HAVE WRITTEN:

Planet Coruscant
Sounds a bit pessimistic
Call it "CorusCAN"

Jedi still wear robes
Even when it is daytime.
They are just lazy.

Cute furry Ewoks
Using my helmet for WHAT?
For a DRUM?? Aw, man . . .

28

_____

_____

_____

_____

_____

_____

_____

_____

_____

NOW TRY WRITING YOUR OWN
HAIKU! REMEMBER: FIVE
SYLLABLES FOR THE FIRST LINE,
THEN SEVEN SYLLABLES FOR THE
SECOND LINE, THEN FIVE ONCE
MORE FOR THE THIRD LINE.

SPECIES SEARCH

CAN YOU FIND THE FOLLOWING ALIEN SPECIES IN THE WORD
SEARCH ON THE NEXT PAGE?

A	F	D	L	I	J	K	B	D	K	H
R	Y	O	B	S	V	P	N	X	R	F
N	J	N	A	I	R	A	D	Y	O	T
A	G	H	U	R	G	S	Q	H	D	G
M	F	B	I	N	H	S	H	T	I	B
J	S	Z	U	G	D	I	O	I	A	D
K	V	G	R	A	N	D	D	F	N	U
B	A	E	R	J	U	G	F	B	H	F
V	R	W	I	K	U	G	H	B	H	D

SICK SITH BURNS

THE EMPEROR OFTEN ENCOURAGES US TO SEE HOW MANY "SICK BURNS" WE CAN COME UP WITH AT THE JEDI'S EXPENSE. HERE ARE A FEW ON THE NEXT PAGES . . .

Yoda is so old,
he helped name
the planets.

"X-wing fighters?"
More like "yecch-wing fighters!"

Q: Why did Yoda cross the road?
A: Because somebody threw him! Get it?
He's tiny!

Yoda is so old, when he was born the *Millennium Falcon* was just the *Two-day-old Falcon*.

Q: How do you make a Jedi burn his ear?

A: Call him when he's ironing.

"Han Solo"?
More like
"Han So-lame"!

33

COMMANDER'S CODE*

AS AN EXERCISE TO KEEP YOUR SKILLS SHARP, YOUR COMMANDER HAS ENCODED A MESSAGE HE RECEIVED FROM ONE OF YOUR FELLOW ROOKIE STORMTROOPERS. IT'S UP TO YOU TO CRACK THE CODE! ON THE NEXT PAGE, FILL IN THE BLANKS USING THE CODE TO REVEAL THE OTHER STORMTROOPER'S MESSAGE!

* NOT TO BE CONFUSED WITH THE CLONE TROOPER KNOWN AS "COMMANDER CODY"

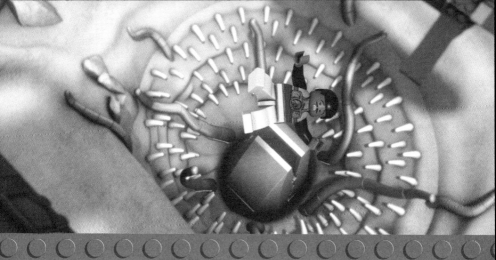

20 8 5   19 1 18 12 1 3 3   16 9 20

1 20 5   13 25   8 15 13 5 23 15 18 11

THE CODE:

A=1 B=2 C=3 D=4 E=5 F=6 G=7 H=8 I=9 J=10 K=11
L=12 M=13 N=14 O=15 P=16 Q=17 R=18 S=19 T=20
U=21 V=22 W=23 X=24 Y=25 Z=26

100% EMPIRE-APPROVED, IMPERIALLY SANCTIONED JOKES PART 2!

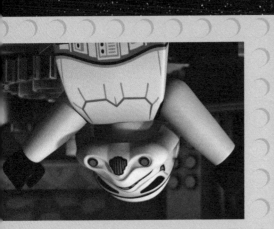

Q: Why do space slugs hate eating Wookiees?

A: They're too CHEWIE!

Q: What did the stormtrooper say to the battle droid?

A: "Why the long face?"

Q: Why did the chicken cross the road?

A: To get to the dark side!

Q: Where do Sith buy their robes?

A: At the Darth Mall

Q: What kind of hot dogs do Jawas eat?

A: Tattoo-weenies

STORMTROOPER POETRY
PART 2

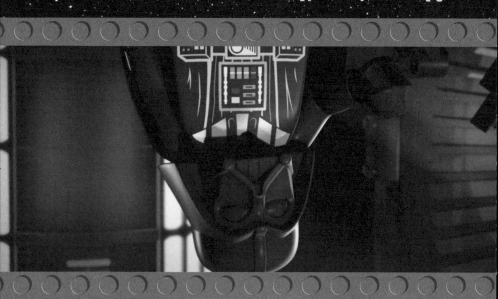

Always two, there are!
One master and apprentice.
Kinda lonely, no?

Scary Palpatine
What they should totes call him is
Sith Lord Crankypants.

Jabba the Hutt is
Hungry all the time, and he
Ate all my pizza.

I went to space jail
And I met Boba Fett there.
He smells like bacon.

Food on the Death Star
Is pretty okay, I guess.
There is no ice cream.

39

MAKE YOUR OWN
STORMTROOPER STORY

WHAT HAPPENED WHEN THE STORMTROOPERS TRIED TO CATCH THE *MILLENNIUM FALCON*? YOU DECIDE! FILL IN THE BALLOONS ON THE NEXT PAGES TO MAKE YOUR OWN COMIC! NOTE THAT ONE OF YOUR TROOPER BUDDIES MIGHT HAVE FILLED IN SOME TO GET YOU STARTED . . .

41

43

THE END

ANSWERS

NOW IS THE MOMENT OF TRUTH! DO YOU HAVE WHAT IT TAKES TO JOIN THE EMPIRE?

CHECK YOUR ANSWERS ON THESE PAGES.

PAGE 9, MYSTERIOUS MISSING LETTERS

HERA
EZRA
SABINE
ZEB
KANAN
CHOPPER

PAGE 17, SUM-TROOPER

LINE ONE: 13 + 4 + 3
LINE TWO: 8 + 2 + 10
LINE THREE: 9 + 6 + 5

PAGE 20, TROOPER TRIVIA!

1: B) JANGO FETT
2: D) BUILT-IN SHIELD GENERATOR
3: B) EMPEROR PALPATINE
4: D) DO ABSOLUTELY NOTHING WEIRD
5: C) DARTH NASTYUS
6: A) KAMINO

PAGE 24, DECODE THE REBELLION!
CHEWBACCA NEEDS NEW FUR SHAMPOO! —HAN SOLO

PAGE 29, SPECIES SEARCH

A	F	D	L	I	J	K	B	D	K	H
R	Y	O	B	S	V	P	N	X	R	F
N	J	N	A	I	R	A	D	Y	O	T
A	G	H	U	R	G	S	Q	H	D	G
M	F	B	I	N	H	S	H	T	I	B
J	S	Z	U	G	D	I	O	I	A	D
K	V	G	R	A	N	D	D	F	N	U
B	A	E	R	J	U	G	F	B	H	F
V	R	W	I	K	U	G	H	B	H	D

PAGE 34, COMMANDER'S CODE
THE SARLACC PIT ATE MY HOMEWORK

RISE, MY FRIEND! THIS BRINGS US TO THE END OF THE ACTIVITY SECTION. ADD UP THE NUMBER OF ANSWERS YOU GOT RIGHT. WAS YOUR NUMBER ZERO OR LARGER? THEN YOU'RE IN! WELCOME TO THE EMPIRE!

END TRANSMISSION